First Second

New York & London

Text and illustrations copyright © 2010 by Ben Hatke

Published by First Second
First Second is an imprint of Roaring Brook Press, a division of Holtzbrinck Publishing
Holdings Limited Partnership
175 Fifth Avenue, New York, New York 10010

Distributed in the United Kingdom by Macmillan Children's Books, a division of Pan
Macmillan.

Cover and interior design by Colleen AF Venable

Cataloging-in-Publication Data is on file at the Library of Congress

Paperback ISBN: 978-1-59643-446-2
Hardcover ISBN: 978-1-59643-695-4

First Second books are available for special promotions and premiums.
For details, contact: Director of Special Markets, Holtzbrinck Publishers.

First Edition February 2010

Printed in China by South China Printing Co. Ltd.,
Dongguan City, Guangdong Province

Paperback: 10 9 8 7 6 5
Hardcover: 10 9 8 7 6

ZITA THE SPACEGIRL

by Ben Hatke

Book one:

Far From Home

:01

First Second

New York & London

There are two ways of getting home; and one of them is to stay there.

The other is to walk round the whole world till we come back to the same place.

— G.K. Chesterton

THAT WAS IN THE METEOROID?

WHAT DO YOU THINK IT DOES?

PUT IT BACK, ZITA.

I THINK WE SHOULD PUSH THE BUTTON!

WHAT!?! NO!

COME ON, WHAT DO YOU THINK WILL HAPPEN?

SERIOUSLY, PUT IT BACK!

aak! LET GO OF ME!

chapter
two

where...

PANT
PANT

JOOOSEPH!

?!?

RAH! GBBN·RAH!

WHOA! SORRY! I'M SORRY.

TWO ARMS TWO LEGS? ANYONE?

STEP ON UP! ONLY THREE DAYS LEFT! THREE! GET OFF-WORLD WHILE YOU CAN!

THREE DAYS?

eh?

You said "THREE DAYS." WHAT'S THAT MEAN?

GEEZ, WHERE YOU BEEN, KID?

THOSE WITH CASH IS GETTIN' OUT WHILE THEY CAN.

YOU GOT CASH, KID?

NO? THEN GET BACK TO THE TATTERS WHERE YOU BELONG!

LET GO OF ME!

JOSEPH?

THOOM!

PSSSSSSSH!

WAIT!

THE GATEWAY!

WHERE ARE THEY TAKING HIM?

SCOOP
SCOOP

1011001!

ROLFIN' GOF! TOF ROGGLE BORF!

10110! 0110!

ROF!

SPAK
SPAK
SPAK!

UP.

TH-THANKS.

Strong-Strong Helpful.

But not so clever.

HELPFUL'S GOOD.

SO WHERE ARE WE GOING?

Safer for lost girl in alley.

not busy.

down for you.

Pieces of you egg.

RIGHT.

UM, STRONG-STRONG? I'M LOOKING FOR MY FRIEND WHO WAS TAKEN AWAY.

I DON'T THINK I CAN FIND HIM WITH-OUT HELP.

So I WAS KIND OF WONDERING —

THERE YOU ARE, *OAF!*

YOU 'AV ANY IDEA 'OW LONG I BEEN LOOKING, YOU **UGLY BRUTE?**

boss.

30

YOU FINK AWL DAT CARGO'S GOIN' LOAD ISSELF?

YOU FINK YOU ON 'OLIDAY?

YOU WASE AFF THE DAY YOU GET AFF THE PAY!

NOW GET BACK TO THE SHIP, **LUMMOX!**

BOSS.

STRONG-STRONG—

AN' WHERE D'YE FINK YOU'RE GOIN' YE FILFY URCHIN?

MY EMPLOYEES' TIME IS MY TIME. **GOT IT?!?**

NOW BACK TO THE SLUMS WIF YE BEFORE I CALLS THE CONSTABULATORY!

SALTWATER TOO, THAT MEANS **RUST**.

RUST!?! WHAT'R WE GONNA DO?

HOW MANY TIMES I GOTTA EXPLAIN IT, JERRY?

TO FIX THIS SORTA LEAK ALL YOU GOTTA DO IS TELL IT **GOOD NEWS!**

OH, RIGHT!

IN THREE DAYS AN **ASTEROID** IS GONNA **EXPLODE US ALL!**

WHAT.

THAT WAS **BAD NEWS**, JERRY.

PLINK!

34

BUCK-
BUCK!

BUMP

HEY!

CLUCK!

GATHER AROUND
NOW!

GATHER AROUND FOR
THE OPPORTUNITY
OF A LIFETIME.

GOBBLE GOBBLE!

RIP!

YOU SEE?

WITH PIPER'S PATENTED MUSCLE MACHINE YOU CAN BE THE "CREAM OF THE CROP"!

THE COST IS JUST TWO BARRELS OF STAR FUEL.

JUST TWO BARRELS. DON'T BE SHY NOW.

KLUCK?

FLOBBLE

BUCK-*BUCK!?!*

HEH HEH. OF COURSE PERMANENT RESULTS REQUIRE RIGOROUS EXERCISE AND, AH...

ONE BARREL! ONLY ONE BARREL!

GRR...

B-*CAW!*

KICK

HEY!

38

CHICKENS!

BU- CAW!

GULP

TAP TAP

TAP TAP

GASP!

MOUSE!

PIPER'S SONG

I NEED YOU TO SET UP THE COT.

WE HAVE A HOUSE GUEST.

CHIK CHIK!

NO, STILL NO FUEL.

BUT DON'T WORRY-

I THINK WE'RE ONTO SOMETHING.

chapter
three

CHIRP!

CHIRP CHIRP!

SKWAK!

CHOMP CHOMP!

NOT A DREAM THEN.

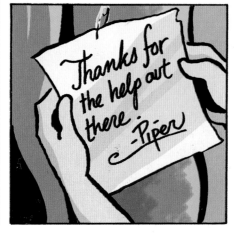

Thanks for
the help out
there. -Piper

45

Sniff

floof

ha!

SKRITCHa
SKRITCH

SKRTCH

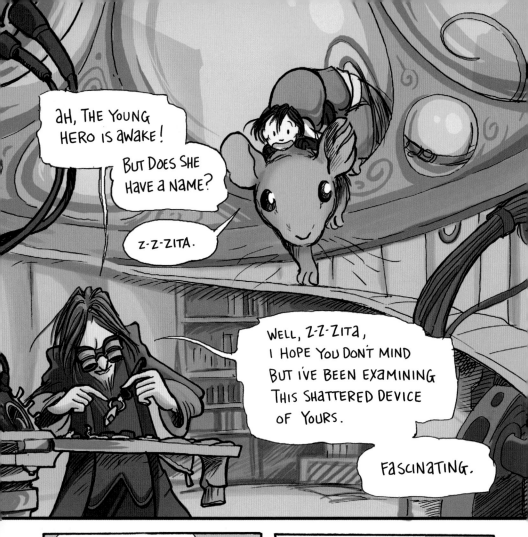

AH, THE YOUNG HERO IS AWAKE!

BUT DOES SHE HAVE A NAME?

Z-Z-ZITA.

WELL, Z-Z-ZITA, I HOPE YOU DON'T MIND BUT I'VE BEEN EXAMINING THIS SHATTERED DEVICE OF YOURS.

FASCINATING.

CAN YOU FIX IT?

WE'LL KNOW IN A MOMENT.

IS THIS YOUR MOUSE? WHAT'S HIS NAME?

OH, HE'S NOT MINE.

HIS REAL NAME IS **PIZZICATO,** BUT HE HATES IT.

CHING!

So I JUST CALL HIM "MOUSE."

HE STARTED TRAVELING WITH ME A FEW WORLDS BACK,

TILL WE GOT STUCK HERE.

I THINK HE'S ON THE RUN.

DID YOU INVENT ALL THESE THINGS?

HM? A FEW OF THEM.

PINK!

MOSTLY I JUST COLLECT AND REFURBISH VINTAGE ITEMS.

HOP!

BOOM!

ARE YOU **CRAZY?!?**

THOSE ARE HOPPIN-STOMP CLASSICS!

THEY'RE A COLLECTOR'S ITEM!

AND YOU **NEVER** WEAR THEM INSIDE!

NOW TRY NOT TO TOUCH ANYTHING ELSE WHILE I –

WHILE I...

GOOD HEAVENS.

WHAT IS IT?

YOUR DEVICE WAS POWERED BY A JUMP CRYSTAL.

I THOUGHT THEY HAD ALL BEEN DESTROYED.

CAN IT SEND ME HOME?

THERE'S NOT MUCH POWER LEFT, BUT—

ZITA, IF I CAN RECREATE THIS DEVICE, I THINK I CAN OPEN A PORTAL LONG ENOUGH TO GET ALL THREE OF US OFF-WORLD BEFORE THE ASTEROID HITS.

I'D HAVE TO LEAVE MY SHIP BEHIND, BUT—

NO.

WHAT?

I'M SORRY, PIPER.

I CAME HERE LOOKING FOR MY FRIEND JOSEPH.

HE WAS KIDNAPPED BECAUSE OF ME.

I CAN'T GO HOME WITHOUT HIM.

WELL, THAT DOES COMPLICATE THINGS, DOESN'T IT, MOUSE?

SKWIK!

CAN YOU DESCRIBE THE CREATURE THAT TOOK YOUR FRIEND?

POOM!

WELL, HE HAD A HELMET AND THESE UGLY TENTACLES.

YOU KNOW, THAT ACTUALLY DOESN'T NARROW IT DOWN MUCH.

HERE, I'LL MAKE A LIST OF PAGES INDEXED FOR BOTH "HELMET" AND "TENTACLES."

YOU SEE IF YOU CAN FIND A MATCH.

SIGH

Dozer

...f several species which
...ate from the planet called
..., the industrious Dozers are
...y sought after as builders,
...tects and foremen on
... renovation projects.
...ers hatch fully formed
...cemented egg
...

Whiskersmith

...as composers
...the armless
...sters sport a
...beard-like
...h. They
...travel
...ly stray
...ir home
...ba, and
...y-seven
...g moons.

Tentacled Tubb

...n without a
...g televisor,
...seen
...habitable
...and video
...ions.
...y
...ation
...cled
...w

IT'S HIM.

PIPER! PIPER! I FOUND HIM!

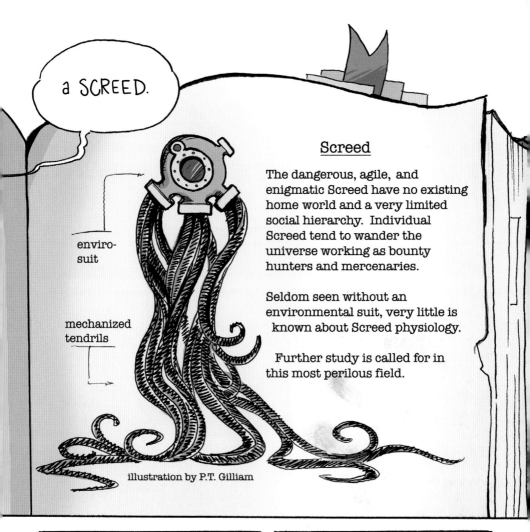

a SCREED.

Screed

The dangerous, agile, and enigmatic Screed have no existing home world and a very limited social hierarchy. Individual Screed tend to wander the universe working as bounty hunters and mercenaries.

Seldom seen without an environmental suit, very little is known about Screed physiology.

Further study is called for in this most perilous field.

enviro-suit

mechanized tendrils

illustration by P.T. Gilliam

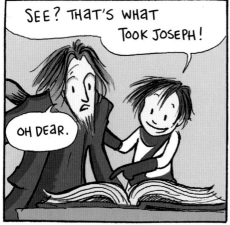

SEE? THAT'S WHAT TOOK JOSEPH!

OH DEAR.

YOUR FRIEND IS IN TERRIBLE DANGER.

PLINK!

PLINK!

PLINK!

URK!

P-PIPER!

PLINK!

HI THERE, JERRY.

LISTEN, I NEED THE KEY TO MAINTENANCE TUNNEL 42.

I-I...

TIME TO PAY THE PIPER, JERRY.

J-J-JES' DON'T TELL NOBODY.

KLINK!

YOUR FRIEND HAS BEEN CAPTURED BY THE SCRIPTORIANS.

THE PLANET'S FIRST INHABITANTS.

CLIK
K-CHANK

WHEN THE ASTEROID WAS SPOTTED, EVERYONE RUSHED TO EVACUATE.

BUT NOT THE SCRIPTORIANS.

THEY JUST- NGH! - LOCKED THEMSELVES IN A CASTLE WITH THAT **SCREED** RUNNING THEIR ERRANDS.

I CAN'T IMAGINE A WORSE PLACE TO BE.

WELL, IN YOU GO.

WHAT?

THIS TUNNEL LEADS TO THE EDGE OF TOWN.

FROM THERE YOU CAN PICK UP THE TRAIL THAT RUNS THROUGH THE RUSTED WASTES,

AND RIGHT TO SCRIPTORIAN CASTLE.

YOU AREN'T COMING?

I'M STAYING BEHIND TO REPAIR YOUR JUMPGATE.

I'LL CATCH UP WHEN I CAN.

SO, ARE YOU SURE ABOUT THIS?

GULP!

ACTUALLY, I—

CHIK CHIK!

ALL RIGHT! OKAY!

I CAN'T STOP YOU!

MOUSE?

HE THINKS YOU'LL MAKE BETTER TIME WITH HIS HELP.

OH MOUSE! THANK YOU!

flip

YOU KNOW, NONE OF THE CREATURES WE'VE SEEN ARE IN THIS BOOK.

CH-CHING!

YOU'RE RIGHT! THERE'S NO ENTRY FOR GIANT MICE EITHER!

WHACK CRACK!

WHACK and SMACK!

RAAH! CEASE THIS TORMENT, YOU WRETCHED JACKANAPES!

SPANG!

PANG!

a THWACK!

HEY!

GO ON, BEAT IT!

AAK! TRICK AND KICK!

YES! WATCH THEM RUN!

LOOK! ONE OF THEM HAS TRIPPED! IF YOU ACT QUICKLY YOU CAN STOMP HIM!

WHAT?!?

BAH! IN YOUR SLOTH YOU HAVE ALLOWED HIM TO ESCAPE.

BUT I DON'T WANT TO STOMP THOSE LITTLE GUYS!

PRESERVING YOUR FINE BOOTS NO DOUBT.

IF YOU RELEASE ME I COULD VAPORIZE THE "LITTLE GUYS" FOR YOU!

WHAT?!? WHAT KIND OF CREATURE ARE YOU?

I AM A HEAVILY ARMORED MOBILE BATTLE ORB.

A WARRIOR ROBOT, THE LAST OF MY KIND.

H.A.M.B.O.?

THAT ACRONYM IS UNDIGNIFIED!

I PREFER MY NUMERICAL DESIGNATION:

ONE!

WELL ALL RIGHT THEN, ONE. IT WAS NICE MEETING YOU.

WH-WHAT? YOU WOULD LEAVE ME TO MY DOOM?

YOU WERE OBVIOUSLY LEFT THERE FOR A REASON.

...YES.

"FAILURE TO WORK WELL WITH OTHERS."

SO YOU **ARE** DANGEROUS.

IT IS TRUE — I WAS BUILT FOR **GLORIOUS COMBAT!**

BUT EVEN I DRAW THE LINE AT CAPTURING CHILDREN.

CAPTURING CHILDREN?

THE ONE WE CAUGHT WAS PASTY AND SOFT— OBVIOUSLY ONE OF YOUR SPECIES.

WE WERE TO BRING HIM TO THE SCRIPTORIANS FOR SOME KIND OF **SACRIFICE.**

CLICK

PSHHHHH

FREEDOM.

FREEDOM!

FREEDOM!

CLAK
CLAK

THERE IS A LARGE RODENT BEHIND YOU.

WHAT?!?

YOU CAN'T HURT MOUSE!

PUT THAT THING AWAY!

CLAK CLAK

COME ON— WE STILL HAVE A LONG WAY TO GO.

THEN WE RIDE TOGETHER TO MAKE OUR FINAL STAND.

chapter
four

NGH

YOUR PROGRESS
HAS SLOWED
CONSIDERABLY.

CLIMBING
IS HARD
WORK, ONE.

I DO NOT
FIND IT
CHALLENGING.

THAT'S NOT CLIMBING!

PERHAPS YOU
SHOULD INSTALL
HOVER UNITS
ON YOUR
RODENT.

NG

Pff

sniff

THIS PLACE IS UNHYGIENIC.

ROBOTS WORRY ABOUT THAT?

...

RRRR...

RRRRR...

-DOOM!

I SUGGEST WE PROCEED WITH CAUTION.

STCH.

I'VE NEVER SEEN A JUNKYARD LIKE THIS.

HNH.

IT USED TO BE A CITY.

WHAT HAPPENED?

ARE YOU SURE YOU WANT TO KNOW?

THE SCRIPTORIANS DESTROYED IT.

IN AN EFFORT TO DESTROY THE ASTEROID THEY BUILT A WEAPON OF UNFATHOMABLE POWER.

BUT THEY COULD NOT CONTROL IT.

AND IT DESTROYED THIS PLACE.

AND THAT'S WHY THEY HOLED UP IN A CASTLE?

YES.

NOW THEY HAVE THE FOOL IDEA THAT THEY CAN ATONE FOR THEIR MISTAKE BY SACRIFICING YOUR FRIEND.

BUT THEY DIDN'T COUNT ON YOU NOBLY PLUNGING THROUGH THE PORTAL TO SAVE HIM!

IT WASN'T LIKE THAT, ONE.

BUT WHAT ABOUT THE WEAPON?

LOST.

PROBABLY BURIED DEEP WITHIN THESE RUINS.

BUT DO NOT WORRY.

I AM SURE THERE ARE OTHER DANGERS IN THIS WASTE.

SKTCH!

YES! NOW OUR HEAT INDEX WILL REMAIN **OPTIMUM** THROUGH THE NIGHT!

ZITA?

THE CONSTELLATIONS ARE GONE.

CONSTELLATIONS?

PICTURES YOU CAN SEE IN THE STARS.

ORION, CASSIOPEIA, THE BIG DIPPER.

YOU COULD SEE THEM FROM ANYWHERE ON EARTH.

YOU ARE MANY THOUSANDS OF LIGHT YEARS FROM HOME. STAR PATTERNS CHANGE AS YOU MOVE THROUGH SPACE.

YEAH **THANKS,** ONE.

JUST WHAT I NEEDED TO HEAR!

SKTCH

SKRRRRCH!
CLIK
CLIK
CLIK

WEAPON SYSTEMS ONLINE.

TAKE YOUR REST, ZITA.

I WILL KEEP WATCH THROUGH THE NIGHT.

So there we were, locked in mortal combat—

Are you going to help find the trail, or WHAT?

Clearly you don't appreciate a good story.

We're LOST, One! Not the best time for memoirs.

CLAK CLAK

SKTCH...

Easy, Mouse.

aaH!

JUST LOOK!
THE POOR THING IS
SCARED TO
DEATH!

BITS FALL
OFF.

HEY THERE, DON'T
BE AFRAID.

DO YOU HAVE
A NAME?

R-RANDY.

NO WONDER YOU HAVE A
HARD TIME WALKING.
THESE ARE RUSTED THROUGH.

I'M ON MY
LAST LEGS.

THERE'S LOTS OF
PARTS AROUND
HERE,

MAYBE WE
CAN RIG
SOMETHING
UP.

YOU KNOW I ONCE
FACED OFF AGAINST
A TOLGOTHIAN
BATTLE MECH.

CHIK
CHIK!

aaand...

DONE.

HOW'S THAT FEEL?

A LITTLE TIPSY.

...AND THEN I SAID TO THREE "HA! YOU ONLY THINK YOU'VE DEFEATED ME!" AND I –

SQUIGGA SKWEE

SQUIGGA SKWEE! SQUIGGA SKWEE!

GUYS, THIS IS ROBOT RANDY. HE'S BEEN LIVING HERE FOR AGES BUT NOW HE WANTS TO JOIN US!

I HAVE THE SQUEAKS.

THIS WAY.

YOU SEE, ONE? HE'S A PERFECT GUIDE.

HNH.

SQUIGGA-SKWEE!

SQUIGGA SKWEE!

SKWEE
SQUIGGA-SKWEE!
SQUIGGA SKWEE!
SQUIGGA SKWEE! SQUIGGA

YOU DO NOT THINK HIS INCESSANT **SQUEAKING** WILL DRAW UNWANTED ATTENTION?

WHAT COULD HAPPEN?

SKRRCH!!

CLIK CLIK CLIK

WHAT'S THAT?

MECHANIZED PREDATORS.

WE'RE BEING HUNTED.

SKTCH
SKTCH

CLAK
CLAK

SKREEE!

MOUSE?

SKREEK!

MOUSE, NO!

ONE! DO SOMETHING!

JAMMED!

CLAK   CLAK

≡KLIKLIKLIK≡

ONE!

M·MY RULE IS...

NO TIPPING.

CHEATER.

SOME KIND OF
ENERGY SURGE...

KLIKLIKLIKLIKLIKLI CHAK≡

THERE
IT GOES.

SKITTR!

SKITTR!

SKITTR!

SKiiiiD!

IT LOOKS LIKE I CAUGHT UP JUST IN TIME.

WHOa!

PIPER!

I BELIEVE YOU ALREADY KNOW HOW TO USE THESE.

HUFF
HUFF

SHIK!

ZZT!
ZZT!

MOUSE!

sniff
sniff

PIPER'S NOT GOING TO LIKE THIS.

COME ON, MOUSE, LET'S GET THESE WEBS OFF YOU.

THERE WE ARE, RIGHT AS RAIN.

LOOKS LIKE OUR YOUNG SPACEGIRL HAS BEEN MAKING FRIENDS.

I'M NOT RELIABLE.

101

ZZZ

SQUIGGA SKWEE!

SQUIGGA SKWEE!

SQUIGGA SKWEE!

LET ME TAKE A LOOK AT THAT.

SKITTR!

THERE.

THAT SHOULD FIX THE SQUEAKING...

BUT I DON'T KNOW WHAT'S CAUSING THE RATTLING.

NERVES.

I'VE NEVER BEEN THIS FAR FROM THE SCRAP PILES BEFORE.

WE'RE NEARING THE EDGE OF THE RUSTED WASTES—THE CASTLE IS JUST OVER THAT HILL.

THERE.

NOW DO YOU UNDERSTAND HOW DIFFICULT THIS REALLY IS?

BUT - BUT WE STILL HAVE TO TRY!

DON'T WE?

YOU FIXED IT.

YES, BUT I DISCOVERED SOMETHING IN THE PROCESS.

THE CRYSTAL HAS KEYED ITSELF TO YOUR GENETIC CODE. ONLY YOU CAN PUSH THIS BUTTON.

PLEASE, ZITA.

LET'S ESCAPE THIS WORLD WHILE WE STILL CAN.

B-DOW!

YOU SEE, THE SECRET IS TO SAUTÉ THE VEGETABLES IN ADVANCE.

ANOTHER LITTLE STEPPING STONE -

ON THE ROAD TO **MAJESTY.**

M-MAJESTY MAKES ME SHAKE.

AIEEE!

ZITA?

HAND OVER THE GIRL.

DESTROYING THE DEVICE WAS **NOT** PART OF THE AGREEMENT.

AGREEMENT?

PIPER, WHAT DOES HE MEAN??

I'M SORRY, ZITA.

WALK AWAY WHILE YOU CAN, MINSTREL.

YOU WILL FIND YOUR SHIP FUELED.

DO NOT STRUGGLE HUMAN CHILD.

NOT SO FAST.

DON'T WORRY, ZITA. I WILL PROTECT YOU.

WELL, WELL, WELL. IF IT ISN'T LITTLE **ONE!**

F-FIVE?

EIGHT?

BKAW BKAW!

KLIKA PTOO!

I'LL HANDLE THIS, EIGHT.

PLINK!

WAS THAT SUPPOSED TO HURT?

NOT THAT.

THESE.

POOT POOT

UH-OH.

BARNACLE BOMBS!

BOOM!

ZITA?

ONE!

MY-MY FRIENDS!

NOBODY HURTS MY FRIENDS!

SKWIK!

TIME TO DO YOUR PART, EIGHT.

HNH.

GUH!

BUMP.

YOU!

SHH! SHHH!

I TRUSTED YOU, YOU SLIMY **TRAITOR!**

SO WHADDAYA WANNA BET I CAN DRILL RIGHT THROUGH HIS OPTICS?

huh huh.

VRRT!

LEAVE THEM.

WE HAVE WHAT WE CAME FOR.

MAKE WAY!

MAKE WAY! MAKE WAY FOR THE HUMAN CHILD!

NO! I TOLD YOU! I'M NOT WHO YOU THINK!

DRAG
DRAG

!

HSST!
CHIK-CHIK!

ᵒᵒᵒᵒG.

ZZZT!
ZZ!

SCAVENGERS!

D-DON'T
WORRY.
HEE HEE!

THEY'RE F-FIXING US.
HEE HEE!

ZZZT!

ZZT!
ZZZ!

THEY'RE AFRAID OF MOUSE.

REPAIRS...
RETRIBUTION!

YES! WORK QUICKLY, MY LITTLE FRIENDS!

SOON WE WILL BE BATTLE READY!

WH-WHAT WAS TH-THAT?

GRAVITATIONAL TREMORS.

THIS PLANET IS RUNNING OUT OF TIME.

SETTLE DOWN IN THERE!

SPANG SPANG SPANG!

WE HAVEN'T BEEN MAKING NOISE.

YEAH, WE AREN'T EVEN SPEAKING TO EACH OTHER.

ENOUGH! QUIET YOU!

I SEE YOU'RE A MAN WHO TAKES HIS JOB VERY SERIOUSLY.

I'M THE DUNGEON-KEEPER!

AND CERTAINLY AN **IMPOSING** ONE.

OH...

THANK YOU.

LISTEN, MY FRIEND AND I WERE WONDERING —

I'M NOT YOUR FRIEND!

RIGHT. THE YOUNG LADY AND I WERE WONDERING HOW LONG BEFORE...

YOU KNOW...

BOOM!

You mean you've never heard the PROPHECY?

JOSEPH the HUMAN is going to SAVE US!

He came to us just as was FORETOLD!

And in our DARKEST HOUR he will unleash his MYSTICAL POWER and destroy THE SPACE ROCK!

And then the GREAT CELEBRATION BEGINS!

There will be FEASTING and mus- m-mm...

MMM...MM MUSIC...

FLOMP

HEH HEH.

YOU DON'T LOOK VERY IMPRESSED.

Z

YOU KNOW THIS DOESN'T WORK FOR JUST ANYONE.

WHAT?

"WHAT?" WHAT DO YOU MEAN WHAT? THAT GUARD WILL KILL US WHEN HE WAKES UP!

RELAX.

WE WON'T EVEN BE HERE.

WE WON'T?

NOPE.

BECAUSE I BROUGHT THIS.

a-a-are you sure about this?

HUF HUF...

I HAVE ORCHESTRATED 47 PRISON BREAKS ON 12 PLANETS! I WILL DRILL THROUGH THE WALL IN SECONDS.

VRRT!

PLIP!

Y-YOU'RE STILL LEAKING MAINLINE FLUID! Y-YOU'RE GOING TO GO INTO **PERMANENT SHUTDOWN!**

LISTEN RUSTBUCKET, WHEN I WANT YOUR ADVICE I'LL TEAR IT OUT OF YOUR **MAINFRAME!**

THIS IS A **RESCUE MISSION!**

AND NOT ONE WORD ABOUT MY - eh?

CHIK CHIRRIP!

QUICKLY, ZITA! THESE DOORS DON'T LAST LONG.

NGH.

CHIK!

YOU'RE OKAY! HOW DID YOU GUYS FIND ME?

HUF HUF

ONE WAS LOOKING FOR A PLACE TO BLAST THROUGH THE WALL TO R-RESCUE YOU.

AH! THE SWEET BREATH OF FREEDOM!

HA HA! NO PRISON IN THE UNIVERSE CAN HOLD US!

RIGHT, ZITA?

ZITA?

CLAK CLAK

SHALL I RID THE WORLD OF HIM?

LET HIM GO, ONE.

HE CAN RUN BACK TO HIS SHIP — IT'S ALL HE CARES ABOUT.

WE'LL GO FIND JOSEPH.

RIGHT. TA-TA, THEN.

ENJOY YOUR DOOMED PLANET.

135

WHAT, IZZAT THE **BEST** Y' CAN DO?

HANDLE

IZZAT **ALL YOU CAN CARRY?**

PRECIOUS FOODSTUFFS

HANDLE WITH

STRONG-STRONG? PFF! MORE LIKE **WEAK-WEAK!**

aHEM.

eh?

WELL, WELL, WELL. IF IT ain'T THE LITTLE URCHIN.

CRASH!

WH- MY CARGO!

Hi, lost girl!

chapter
five

You okay down there?

NGH. FINE.

You just seem kind of... wobbly.

I said i'm FINE!

RIGHT THIS WAY.

LAST LOAD, TOPPER?

HUH?

OH! YES, GOT THE LAST LOAD HERE ALL RIGHT. HEH HEH.

YOU SEEM CHEERFUL.

I-I DO?

I MEAN, OF COURSE I DO! SOON I'LL BE LEAVING YOUR UGLY PLANET!

HA! THAT'S THE TOPPER I KNOW.

SO WHAT'S IN THE BOX?

OH, IT'S... UM... CAKE?

CAKE? IN THIS SUN?!? GET IT TO STORAGE!

OH, RIGHT! UM, MOVE IT, YOU OAF!

IT'S THEM ALL RIGHT. FIVE AND EIGHT.

OKAY, ONE. I NEED YOU TO DISTRACT THEM WHILE THE REST OF US SLIP BY.

ONE?

H-HIS MAINLINE WAS CUT IN THE LAST FIGHT.

H-HE'S GETTING W-WEAKER.

I ≡COUGH≡ I TOLD YOU WE WERE GOING TO MAKE OUR **FINAL STAND.**

STRONG-STRONG help red ball!

Y-YOU WILL?

YES... YES WE WILL USE THE POWER OF **TEAMWORK!**

I FEEL A SECOND WIND...

ARE YOU BORED?

HM?

I SAID, "ARE YOU BORED?"

oh.

I was thinking about little animals.

You know...

with cute fuzzy faces.

HEH, HEH, YEAH.

SMASHING UP LITTLE ANIMALS IS THE BEST.

LOOK LIVELY, CHUMPS!

BAP

LURCH!

WE'RE NOT MOVING.

THE B-BRAKE CONTROLS — THEY'RE S-S-STUCK!

MOUSE? WHAT ARE YOU DOING?

GNAW!

GNAW!

SNAP!

BOFF

OOF!

149

BAF!

LOOKS LIKE THE **END** FOR YOU, ONE.

YOU'RE ONLY A F-FLUMSY **COPY**, FIVE.

COPY!?! HA! WHY DIDN'T THEY STOP WHEN THEY MADE YOU?

I MEAN, DO YOU HAVE **ANY** IDEA?

IT'S BECAUSE YOU WERE PROGRAMMED WITH **HONOR** AND **LOYALTY**.

HUFF HUFF

THE REST OF US DON'T HAVE THOSE **DEFECTS**.

KEEP TALKING, FIVE. ALL YOU'RE DOING IS—

152

DISTRACTING ME?!?

STRONG-STRONG!

HOMING BEACON!

HEH HEH.

FLING!

UH-OH.

FNIKT

I SUSPECTED YOU WOULD BE TROUBLE.

LOOK HERE.

AH!

THE MYSTICAL ENERGY WILL COME FROM HIS CHEST.

EXTRAORDINARY!

ZITA!

GH...PIPER?

YOU CAME BACK.

YEAH.

NOT SO CLEVER AFTER ALL.

FOOM!

Z-ZITA...

S-SOMETHING'S WRONG.

S-SOMETHING I DIDN'T TELL YOU B-BEFORE.

ABOUT THE WEAPON THAT D-DESTROYED THE CITY.

IT'S ME.

I - I WAS AFRAID IF I TOLD YOU, YOU'D LEAVE ME BEHIND.

ALONE.

I THOUGHT I COULD CONTROL THE WEAPON INSIDE ME.

BUT WHEN I SAW YOU IN DANGER, IT POWERED UP ON ITS OWN.

I CAN'T STOP IT.

YOU SEE, THE PROCESS HAS BEGUN!

AMAZING!

SO BRIGHT!

YOU'RE DOING FINE! JUST AS THE SCROLLS FORETOLD!

WHAT ARE YOU TALKING ABOUT?!? I'M NOT DOING ANYTHING!

RRRRUUUUMBLLLE

RRRRRRRRRUUUUUUMMMMBLE RRUMMMBLLEE

SO.

WE'RE CAUGHT BETWEEN A MALFUNCTIONING ULTIMATE WEAPON AND A DOOMSDAY ASTEROID.

EVEN IF WE WERE ON MY SHIP, THERE'S NO WAY WE COULD LAUNCH IN TIME.

SO THIS IS THE END.

FOR US, YES.

MAYBE NOT FOR YOU.

NOT MANY PEOPLE ESCAPE THE END OF A WORLD.

GO SAVE YOUR FRIEND.

SNRGHT

I WON'T FORGET YOU, PIPER!

THERE IT IS.

MY MISSING PIECE!

MISSING PIECE MISSING PIECE...

OF **COURSE!**

ROBOT RANDY'S WEAPON SYSTEM MUST RELY ON **HATZENFORD POINT ENERGY!**

THE SAME ENERGY THE JUMP CRYSTAL DRAWS ON!

THEY USED THE CRYSTAL AS A FOCUSING DEVICE.

BRILLIANT!

WE JUST REPLACE THE CRYSTAL, POINT HIM TOWARD THE ASTEROID, AND—

AAAH!

BOOOM!

ZITA.

NNGH.

THE CRYSTAL...
THE BLAST WILL
DESTROY IT.

YOU WONT BE
ABLE TO GO
HOME.

CHINK!

chapter
six

SO THERE WE WERE, STEELY RESOLVE WASHING ACROSS OUR FACES AS WE FACED A HUNDRED WARRIORS.

strong-strong count fifteen.

AND YOU FOUGHT THEM ALL OFF BEFORE SHUTTING DOWN?

IT WAS NOTHING, YOUNG JOSEPH. HAVE I EVER TOLD YOU ABOUT THE TIME I—

MORE QUIET for lost girl!!

CHIK CHIK!

YOU'RE ALL HERE!

THANKS TO YOU.

PIPER TOLD ME EVERYTHING YOU WENT THROUGH TO FIND ME.

YEAH. WELL...

MASTER JOSEPH! OH, MASTER JOSEPH!

OH NO! IT'S **THEM!**

MASTER JOSEPH? ARE YOU—

AH! THE FRIEND OF MASTER JOSEPH IS AWAKE!

UM. HELLO.

IS THERE ANYTHING YOU REQUIRE? ANY FRIEND OF MASTER JOSEPH IS OUR REVERED AND HONORED GUEST!

UM...

I'M FINE. MAYBE YOU SHOULD KEEP LOOKING FOR JOSEPH.

HE COULD BE LOST IN THE CASTLE!

HOW **THOUGHTFUL!** MASTER JOSEPH HAS THE FINEST FRIENDS.

WE BOW **LOW!**

WHAT WAS THAT ABOUT?

THEY WANT TO MAKE ME KING!

OF THEIR WHOLE PLANET!

YIKES.

I IMAGINE YOU WILL RULE WISELY.

THINK OF IT, JOSEPH— POWER, MAJESTY!

G-GOLD CROWNS CAN CAUSE A R-RASH.

YOUR ENEMIES PROSTRATE BEFORE YOU!

BUT I DON'T WANT ANY OF THAT.

I JUST WANT TO GO HOME.

URM.

SHUFFLE

ABOUT SENDING YOU KIDS HOME,

LISTEN...

THE BLAST THAT DESTROYED THE ASTEROID SAVED — THIS WORLD,

BUT IT SHATTERED THE CRYSTAL.

THIS SHARD IS ALL THAT'S LEFT.

NOW THE GOOD NEWS, OF COURSE—

IS THAT I'M A GENIUS.

I'VE MODIFIED THE ORIGINAL DEVICE TO WORK WITH THE REMAINING SHARD,

BUT THE BAD NEWS...

THE BAD NEWS IS THAT THE PORTAL WILL BE VERY UNSTABLE. SO YOU SHOULD GO NOW. NO LONG GOODBYES— AND NO PROMISES.

Strong-Strong will go!

ooOoh.

THEN WE SHOULD SLIP OUT OF THE CASTLE BEFORE THOSE SCRIPTORIANS COME BACK.

BESIDES...

JOSEPH WOULD MAKE A TERRIBLE KING!

BAP

HEY!

YOU READY?

HM?

YEAH. YEAH, I'M READY.

Snif

SOMETHING IN MY EYE.

HERE WE GO.

KLIK!

CHNK!

THOOM!

NO!

NGH!

WHAT'S HAPPENING?

THE PORTAL IS DESTABLIZING!

ONE OF YOU HAS TO LET GO!!

ZITA?

HE MADE IT.

JOSEPH'S HOME.

WHAT ABOUT YOU?

YOUR SHIP IS ALL FUELED UP NOW, RIGHT?

YES, BUT...

THEN WHAT ARE WE WAITING FOR?

I'LL JUST HAVE TO TAKE THE LONG WAY HOME.

IN MY SHIP?

HEY WAIT!

Follow Zita's space adventures in
LEGENDS OF ZITA

EARLY ZITA SKETCHES

I THINK I'VE GOT AN IDEA

I...I'VE GOT AN IDEA.

A SMALL WARRIOR!

A POCKET WARRIOR! EXCELLENT.

I DON'T KNOW... YOU'RE SURE TROLLS ARE AFRAID OF THESE THINGS?

POSITIVE!

ALL TROLLS IS AFEARED OF THE PLUNGAH!

I THINK I'VE DIRTIED YOUR TEACUP.

Pipe

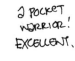

MY FAVORITE FOOD FROM THE MEAT CATEGORY IS SUGAR.

ACKNOWLEDGEMENTS

They say a tale grows in the telling, and it's surely true with this little book, which went through so many changes in its journey to the printed page. There are a lot of people I should thank.

Special thanks go first to my wife Anna for her great patience, never-ending cheerful support, and so much more. And, with her, thanks to all the people who read through early drafts and were willing to say "I don't get it" or "That's not funny"—especially Ryan, Gwen, and Regina.

In a particular way I want to thank the talented Kean Soo who, when all hope was lost, took me back to the beginning and reminded me what was important. And thanks to my stalwart editor Kat Kopit, who kept up with me through trans-Atlantic address changes and shifting phone numbers. And thanks to my agent Judy Hansen, for her eagle eye and patience with the "artistic temperament."

And to the captain of the First Second ship, Mark Siegel, who gave me that final challenge.

And of course to my three daughters, Angelica, Zita, and Julia, who—when their powers combine—form an unruly pack of pure inspiration.

ABOUT THE AUTHOR

Ben Hatke has published comics stories in the Flight series as well as in Explorer. This book is his first full-length graphic novel. It's a first for Zita, too, but she has many more adventures up her sleeve.

Ben lives in Virginia's Shenandoah Valley with his wife, three daughters, twelve chickens, and a cat. He also enjoys juggling, playing his Irish whistle, and occasionally breathing fire. His work can be seen at www.benhatke.com